Be Quiet, Pooh!

Disney's
Winnie the Pooh First Readers

DISNEP'S
A Winnie the Pooh First Reader

Be Quiet, Pooh!

By Isabel Gaines

ILLUSTRATED BY Josie Yee

DISNEP PRESS

NEW YORK

Vivian Lia's Book

Be Quiet, Pooh!

The sun streamed in

through Pooh's window.

"What a happy day!" he said.

Pooh got out of bed.

He stretched up.

He stretched down.

Then, he ate

a big jar of honey.

It was nice outside,

so Pooh decided to take a walk.

While Pooh walked,

he made up a song.

"I had some honey.

Today is so sunny.

Hum, dee, ho, hummy."

9

Soon Pooh came

to Rabbit's house.

"Hum, dee, dee,

dum, dum," Pooh sang.

Rabbit poked his head

out of his window.

"Pooh, you woke

me up!" said Rabbit.

"I'm sorry," said Pooh.

"Would you like to sing with me?"

"No," said Rabbit.

Rabbit slammed his window shut
and went back to bed.

Pooh continued on his walk.

The next day was also

bright and sunny.

Pooh woke up

in a happy mood.

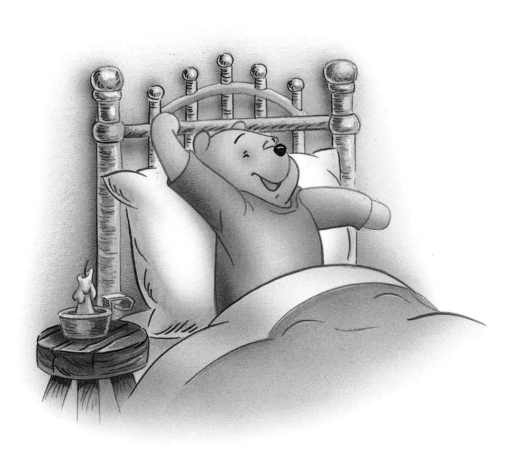

He got out of bed.

He stretched up.

He stretched down.

Then, he ate
a big jar of honey.

Once again,

he went out for a walk.

"The sun is so sunny,

I want more honey," sang Pooh.

When Pooh walked by Rabbit's house,

Pooh saw something new.

"Rabbit has a sign,

and it looks so fine,"

Pooh sang.

"Pooh, you woke me up again!"

shouted a sleepy Rabbit.

"Sorry, Rabbit," said Pooh.

"I like your new sign."

NO SINGING IN THE MORNING

"Thank you," said Rabbit.

"I made it. It says,

NO SINGING IN THE MORNING!"

"You did a very nice job,"

said Pooh.

The next morning,

Pooh decided to walk

in the other direction.

Rabbit slept happily

in his bed until he heard,

"Chirp, chirpety, chirp."

"Is that you, Pooh?" he called.

He looked out his window,

but Pooh was nowhere in sight.

Then Rabbit saw

a bird's nest on the sign.

"Chirp, chirpety, chirp,"

sang the baby birds

in the nest.

"Oh dear," said Rabbit.

He couldn't tell the baby birds

to be quiet.

They were so cute.

Their song was so sweet.

The next morning,

Rabbit awoke once again

to the baby birds singing.

He tried to be mad at them.

But as he listened to their song,

Rabbit discovered he rather liked it.

Then Rabbit heard Pooh

coming down the path.

Pooh was singing, too.

And his song matched

the baby birds' song.

Rabbit got an idea.

He jumped out of bed

and ran outside.

When Pooh arrived
at Rabbit's house,
he noticed Rabbit's sign
was different.

NO
PLEASE
SINGING
IN THE
MORNING

"What happened to your sign?"

asked Pooh.

"I fixed it," said Rabbit.

"Now it says,

PLEASE SING IN THE MORNING."

"What a wonderful idea!"

said Pooh.

"Would you like to join me

in a song or two now?"

"I most certainly would,"

said Rabbit.

And from that day on,

Pooh and Rabbit started every day

with a song.

Can you match the words with the pictures?

honey

bed

head

window

birds

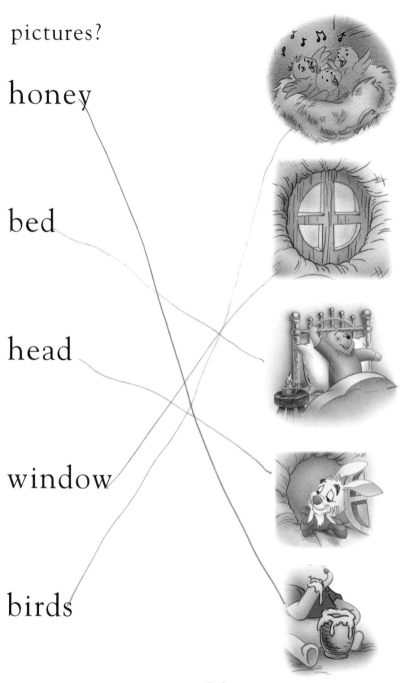

Fill in the missing letters.

sig_n_

R_a_bbit

nes_t_

d_o_wn

pat_h_

37